This book belongs to

★ .... ★

Written by Nick Ellsworth
Illustrated by Veronica Vasylenko

This is a Parragon Publishing Book
First published in 2003
Queen Street House
4 Queen Street
Bath
BA1 1HE, UK

Printed in China
ISBN 1-40541-022-1

THE PRINCESS
and the
MAGIC LOCKET

Written by Nick Ellsworth ★ Illustrated by Veronica Vasylenko

p

It was Princess Crystal's birthday. Her father, the king, had invited everyone to a party at the palace. The king gave Princess Crystal a very special present—a beautiful locket. "This is a magical locket," the king told Princess Crystal. "But it will only work if you say the magic rhyme:

"Magical locket,
Please listen well:
Help my friend
With a kindly spell."

No one noticed the wicked witch peeking through the window. When she saw the magic locket, the witch wanted it for herself.

The next day, Princess Crystal
went riding on her favorite horse.
She didn't see the witch hiding
behind a tree.
As Princess Crystal trotted by,
the wicked witch cast her evil spell:

"Frogs and toads,
And bats of course,
Throw the princess
off her horse!"

Princess Crystal's horse reared up and threw her to the ground.
As quick as a flash, the wicked witch took the locket from around
Princess Crystal's neck.

"Now the locket's mine!" she cackled, and hurried away.

When Princess Crystal opened her eyes, she saw a young prince.

"Are you hurt, Your Highness?" asked the prince.

"I don't think so," said Princess Crystal, sitting up. She felt a bit dizzy from her fall.

"Who are you?" she asked.

"Prince Robert," replied the prince with a smile. "I saw you fall from your horse." When she felt better, Prince Robert gently helped her back onto her horse and led them to the palace gates.

"I shall not forget your kindness," said Princess Crystal. The prince bowed and, turning to wave goodbye, walked back toward the forest.

Meanwhile, the wicked witch
was in her tower, trying to make the
locket's magic work.

"Slimy snails,
And things that lurk,
Make this magical
Locket work!"

She stood back, hoping to see some
magic... but nothing happened.

"Fur of cat,
And eye of bee,
Open the locket's
Secret to me!"

Again, nothing happened.

"Boil and bubble,
And all things bad,
Make it work,
Or I'll go MAD!"

Still nothing happened.
The witch screamed and yelled, and
pulled at her hair and stamped her feet.
All of a sudden, she had an idea.

Meanwhile, Princess Crystal realized that she had lost her magical locket. She decided to ride back to the forest to thank Prince Robert for helping her, and to ask him if he had found the locket.

But the witch was waiting for her up a tree. As soon as Princess Crystal rode by, the witch threw a net over her, bundled the frightened princess over her shoulder, and carried her away.

"I've caught you!" cackled the witch. Soon they arrived at the witch's tower. A fierce dragon guarded it.

"Don't try to escape, my pretty one," said the witch, "or Horace the dragon will eat you up!"

At the top of the tower, the witch freed her.
"Do you remember this?" she asked, holding up the magical locket.
"My locket!" gasped Princess Crystal.
"Yes," hissed the witch. "I stole it from you,
and now I want the magic rhyme to go with it."

"I won't give it to you," said Princess Crystal bravely.
"Then you can stay here until you do!" shouted the witch.
"Here's your precious locket," she said, throwing it at Princess
Crystal. "It won't do you any good locked in here!"
She stormed out of the room, locking the door behind her.

Princess Crystal felt so alone. She leaned out of the window and began to cry. Her tears fell onto Horace the dragon below.

"You're making me all wet," he said grumpily, flying up to the window. "I'm not crying, even though my wing's broken and really hurts."

"Oh, you poor thing," said Princess Crystal, feeling sorry for the dragon. "Maybe I can help you." She closed her eyes, held the locket, and said the magical rhyme:

"Magical locket,
Please listen well:
Help my friend
With a kindly spell."

Princess Crystal opened her eyes, and saw
that Horace's wing had completely healed.
"Oh, thank you," he said happily. "My wing
is healed, and I don't feel grumpy anymore.
But what can I do to return your kindness?"

"Fly to the forest as fast as you can and find help,"
she said. Horace promised he'd go quickly,
and, beating his wings, he rose into the air.

Soon Horace was flying high over the forest.

Horace soon found Prince Robert. As soon as he heard that Princess Crystal had been captured by the witch, he jumped onto Horace's back and flew to the rescue.

As they approached the tower, Prince Robert could see Princess Crystal waving from the tower. Horace flew right up to the window.
"Thank goodness Horace found you," cried Princess Crystal, as Prince Robert climbed in through the window. But before they could escape, the door suddenly opened.

There stood the wicked witch.
"How nice of you to join us,
young man," cackled the witch.
"And how handsome you are!

"But I think you'd look much
better... as a FROG!"
She began to cast an evil spell.

"Oh, no," thought Princess Crystal. "I'd better do something quickly."
She closed her eyes, held the locket, and whispered the magical rhyme:

"Magical locket,
Please listen well:
Help my friend
With a kindly spell."

When Princess Crystal opened her eyes, the locket's magic had worked.

The witch's spell had backfired, and turned her
into a frog instead!
"Frog eggs and slime!" croaked the frog.
Then it hopped out the window, and was never
seen again.

"Thank you, Your Highness," said Prince Robert,
"for saving me from becoming a frog!"
"But you helped me when I fell off my horse, and you
came to rescue me from the witch," said Princess Crystal,
smiling at him. And soon they were flying home.

The king was delighted to see his daughter returned safely. As a reward, the king gave Horace a gleaming new tower.
Princess Crystal and Prince Robert became good friends.

"I'll take care of my precious magical locket forever and ever," Princess Crystal promised.